WELCOME TO
PASSPORT TO READING
A beginning reader's ticket to a brand-new world!

Every book in this program is designed to build read-along and read-alone skills, level by level, through engaging and enriching stories. As the reader turns each page, he or she will become more confident with new vocabulary, sight words, and comprehension.

These PASSPORT TO READING levels will help you choose the perfect book for every reader.

READING TOGETHER
Read short words in simple sentence structures together to begin a reader's journey.

READING OUT LOUD
Encourage developing readers to sound out words in more complex stories with simple vocabulary.

READING INDEPENDENTLY
Newly independent readers gain confidence reading more complex sentences with higher word counts.

READY TO READ MORE
Readers prepare for chapter books with fewer illustrations and longer paragraphs.

This book features sight words from the educator-supported Dolch Sight Words List. This encourages the reader to recognize commonly used vocabulary words, increasing reading speed and fluency.

For more information, please visit lbyr.com/passporttoreading.

Enjoy the journey!

Illustrations by Don Cassity

Cover design by Ching N. Chan. Cover illustration by Don Cassity.

Little, Brown and Company
Hachette Book Group
1290 Avenue of the Americas, New York, NY 10104
Visit us at LBYR.com

First Edition: May 2022

Little, Brown and Company is a division of Hachette Book Group, Inc.
The Little, Brown name and logo are trademarks of Hachette Book Group, Inc.

The publisher is not responsible for websites
(or their content) that are not owned by the publisher.

Library of Congress Control Number 2020933144

ISBNs: 978-0-316-42570-4 (pbk.), 978-0-316-42574-2 (ebook),
978-0-316-42572-8 (ebook), 978-0-316-42573-5 (ebook)

Printed in the United States of America

CW

10 9 8 7 6 5 4 3 2 1

Passport to Reading titles are leveled by independent reviewers applying the standards
developed by Irene Fountas and Gay Su Pinnell in *Matching Books to Readers: Using
Leveled Books in Guided Reading*, Heinemann, 1999.

ILLUMINATION PRESENTS

minions
THE RISE OF GRU

THE SKY IS
THE LIMIT

Adapted by Sadie Chesterfield

Screenplay by Matt Fogel

Illustrated by Don Cassity

LITTLE, BROWN AND COMPANY
New York   Boston

Attention, Minions fans!
Look for these words
when you read this book.
Can you spot them all?

buttons

suitcases

uniforms

snacks

The Minions are having a bad day.

First, they lost the Zodiac Stone.

Next, Gru told them to go away.

Then Gru disappeared!

Bob, Kevin, and Stuart
do not know where Gru is.
What will they do?

The phone rings.

Kevin answers.

It is a bad guy named Wild Knuckles.

"Gru is in San Francisco," he says.

"You have two days to get here
or you are never going to
see your Mini Boss again!"
The Minions need to save Gru!

San Francisco is far away.
Stuart, Bob, and Kevin
put on costumes.
Then they go to the airport.
They need to buy plane tickets.

But they do not have any money!
The Minions try to use
buttons and lint to buy tickets.
That does not work.
How will they get on the plane?

Pilots and flight attendants
walk by the Minions.
They have suitcases
filled with extra uniforms.

The Minions know how they can
get on the plane without tickets.
They grab the suitcases and run.

The Minions put on the uniforms.

Kevin and Stuart look like pilots.

They get on the plane.

Kevin climbs into the pilot's seat.

Stuart is his copilot.

Bob stays with the passengers.

He looks like a flight attendant.

He needs to pass out the snacks.

Kevin reads a book about
how to fly the plane.
How hard can it be?

Stuart pulls a lever.
Kevin tells him to stop,
but Stuart does not listen.

Then Stuart presses a big red button.
The engines turn on.

The plane speeds forward.

Oh no!

It is going to crash
into the buildings!

Kevin pulls back the steering wheel
just in time.
The plane goes up in the air.
It misses the control tower.

Zoom!

Stuart feels sick.

He runs to the bathroom.

Kevin lets the plane fly itself.
It is time for a nap!

He wakes up three hours later
because alarms go off!

Kevin yanks on the controls.
The plane does a loop the loop
before it lands.
They made it to San Francisco!

Stuart was in the bathroom all this time.

Look!

He is covered in toilet paper!

The Minions go to Wild Knuckles's Lair.

Three men guard the door.

They want to stop the Minions.

"Get them!" one man yells.
The men chase the Minions
down an alley.

Master Chow arrives
to help.

She is a kung fu master.

She uses her kung fu to stop the men.

The Minions ask Master Chow
to train them in kung fu.

Master Chow says yes.
She teaches them
some of the basics.

The Minions are ready to go
back to Wild Knuckles's lair.
Will they save Gru?